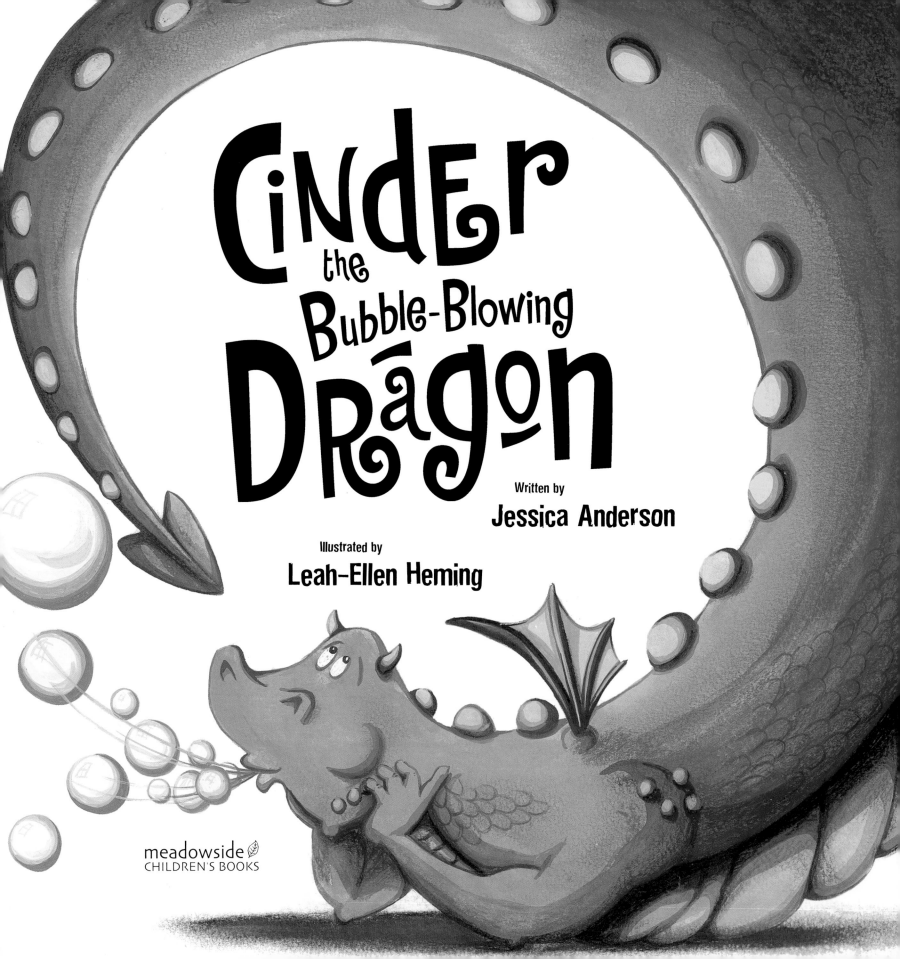

Cinder
the
Bubble-Blowing
Dragon

Written by
Jessica Anderson

Illustrated by
Leah-Ellen Heming

meadowside
CHILDREN'S BOOKS

"This simply won't do," said the King. "You'll have to go."

He shook his head so hard that his crown toppled over one eye. But Cinder, the King's Dragon, didn't dare to smile.

"What sort of dragon are you, anyway?" the King continued. "All the other kings have proper fire-breathing dragons while I, KING OF TARRAGONIA, have a dragon who can only blow...

...bubbles!

The King was right,
thought Cinder.

He was a sad
disappointment.

Coming from a famous dragon
family, great things had been
expected of him.

But when he became the junior dragon at the palace, he found he could only blow bubbles…

…and however hard he **puffed** and **snorted**, not one flicker of flame appeared.

...until he was standing
up to his scaly chest

in one enormous bubble bath.

All the children loved him.

"Blow us some bubbles, Cinder," they would shout whenever they saw him.

They thought bubbles were much better than fire, but the King was not amused.

Now he'd decided that Cinder must go.

He'd even put an advertisement in the **"Tarragonia Times"**.

It read:

One dragon had applied.

"When he comes this afternoon you may be present in the Throne Room to see how a real dragon behaves," said the King.

At two o'clock there was an enormous **roaring** at the palace gates.

"Blaze, the World's Most Fearsome Dragon, wishes to see the King,"
bellowed an enormous voice and the air filled
with smoke and flames.

"OK, OK, show-off, keep your
fireworks for the King," snapped the palace sentry crossly.
He was fond of Cinder and thought it was a shame he had to go.

"Where is the King?" thundered Blaze.
Then, without waiting to be announced,
he stormed into the Throne Room
where the King was seated.
Cinder was crouching miserably
in a corner.

The King looked rather alarmed as the creature's hot breath reached him and frizzled his beard.

Then the carpet started smouldering and flames crept up the curtains

When his crown began to melt the King had had enough.

"**Stop!** he ordered.
"That will do nicely,
thank you."

But Blaze, it seemed, couldn't stop. He was great at starting fires, he explained, but no use at stopping them.

"Cinder, do something," whimpered the King.

Cinder did the only thing he could think of. He blew with all his might and, as the bubbles began to fill the room the flames died down, the carpet no longer smouldered and the Royal Crown stopped melting.

"Now I've done it," thought Cinder.
"I've quite put out Blaze's fire."

Blaze himself was pretty put out too,
but the King was delighted.

"Thank goodness you were here,"
he said, as he ordered a dish of
ice cream to cool himself down.

"Some people don't know what they want – even when they get it," muttered Blaze huffily as he departed in a cloud of very black smoke.

"I don't hold with all this smoke pollution," said the King as he gobbled his ice cream.

"Now,
let's write
another advertisement."

It appeared the next morning
and read:

For Seonaid with love

J.A.

For Mum, Dad, Alex, Anthony,
my dearest friends
and the Kool House

L-E. H.

First published in 2006
by Meadowside Children's Books
185 Fleet Street
London EC4A 2HS

Text © Jessica Anderson 2006
Illustrations © Leah-Ellen Heming 2006
The rights of Jessica Anderson to be
identified as the author
and Leah-Ellen Hemming to be identified
as the illustrator of this work have been
asserted by them in accordance with
the Copyright, Designs and
Patents Act, 1988

A CIP catalogue record for this book
is available from the British Library

ISBN 10 Pbk 1-84539-168-3
ISBN 13 Pbk 978-1-84539-168-3
ISBN 10 Hbk 1-84539-169-1
ISBN 13 Hbk 978-1-84539-169-X

10 9 8 7 6 5 4 3 2 1
Printed in China